The
Witness

The witness

Dr. Sanjay Tota

Edition- jan-2023

notionpress
.com

Index

Introduction

This book is purely inspired from Ashtavakra Geeta. Pure wisdom of life embedded in this sacred texts.

Ashtavakra is traditionally regarded as a sage who lived during ancient times in India. His name, "Ashtavakra," is derived from the legend that he was born with eight physical deformities, symbolising his unique insight and wisdom.

Ashtavakra is best known for his profound teachings on Advaita Vedanta, emphasising the non-dual nature of reality. He engaged in a philosophical dialogue with King Janaka, where he expounded on the nature of the self (Atman) and its identity with Brahman, the ultimate reality. His teachings are recorded in the "Ashtavakra Gita," a scripture that comprises a series of dialogues between Ashtavakra and King Janaka.

Ashtavakra explain one concept to Janaka about drasta , which is heart of this book; Drasta means witness. He said to Janak that you are neither vista nor Spector ; you are just a witness of both.

Ashtavakra's teachings emphasise the importance of self-realization, recognising that the self is beyond the body, mind, and ego. He encourages seekers to transcend dualistic thinking and realise their inherent oneness with the divine.

****

Why are you joined school ? Why are you joined college ? Why are you participated in rate race ? Why are you joined any religion? That's chronological sequence of most of our life ; school, College, job, fitness and religion. We always try to fulfil our life with this life programs and eager to find our saturation in them. After getting it our eyes opens wide; realising that that's not it.

It's purely hoax of our life that something which we don't have we think that if we have that we fulfil our deepest desire. That's on and on. Hope for next best things to come and live our life with utter dissatisfaction with present. Hoax is so permeated in our DNA that if anyone try to explain this we think he is insane. We find saneness in person who is ambitious, man of the match in hoax game!

This dilemma of living life whether you are a farmer or saint prevails in our mind. Saint are in hoax of achievement of meditation milestone and blissfulness. That's nothing else but other polarity of wealth.

***

Our journey start with birth. Quest for satisfaction begin after we have been programme with society, schools and institutions. This book is all about it. May be it's short sentence for you. But important! I believe that like mantra; it will touch you if you open your mind and heart.

"न पुण्यं न पापं न सौख्यं न दुखं
न मंत्रो न तीर्थं न वेदा न यज्ञः
अहं भोजनं नैव भोज्यं न भोक्ता
चिदानंदरूपः शिवोऽहम् शिवोऽहम्"

Means I am Neither virtue nor vice,
neither happiness nor sorrow.
Neither mantra, nor pilgrimage, neither
the Vedas, nor rituals.
I am neither the food, nor the eater, nor
the one who enjoys.
I am of the nature of consciousness and
bliss; I am Shiva, I am Shiva.

The song is a part of a larger philosophical and spiritual text known as the "Nirvana Shatakam" or " Atma Shatakam." This text is attributed to Adi Shankaracharya, an influential Indian philosopher and theologian who lived in the 8th century CE.

The Arrival

PART -1

"The two most important days in your life are the day you are born and the day you find out why."

Mark Twain

After slapped on my back,

I started crying endlessly.

Crying like,

When you reached at one destination ;

suddenly someone grasped you and forced you
into another journey again.

Opening my eyes,

Seeing the most beautiful smile any figure can give ;

I smile back.

Most of the days,

I do two things;

Crying when remembering previous journey

Laughing when I don't.

Astonishing with any sound like

little ring bell, clap and bird chirping;

They widen my eyes fully.

Exhausted frequently ;

Go to sleep anytime

Peace at peak.

Most enjoyable moments of life is when I could not control over things,

Can't hold spoon

Can't sit properly

First step on earth , can't describe ;

If it is first step of beginning

or first step to beginning of a end.

Those time no matter, whenever I fall or slip

Someone there to catch me.

Trust without telling.

Best conversation with all figures;

That is whenever I listen only without any murmured in mind

Not preparing for any answer in mind.

At surprise,

I noted that whenever lip moves the thinking stop.

Now enjoying this symphony ,

Started all things to put in mouth to stop thinking .

Thinking is not hard ;

But habit of avoiding it by any activities primed in me.

There is no time table

Time to eat

Time to sleep

Time to cry.

Everyone thinks that I am mad

But talking with motorbike, teddy and

Pillows.

My routine .

With pen ,

I Scribble great lines

It was so intense that if one can give a pen and paper than I get into flow .

Curiousness is at the peak

What is in drawer?

How to use pen?

How to open door?

Too much forgetful;

Can not remember the enemies

Who don’t give a candy the day before .

So much carelessness

No worries about next meal, place or clothes.

I am walking ;

Just walking .

nothing is more important in that moments than walking

The best days are those

Living in moments to moments .

The Preparation

PART -2

"The day you teach the child the name of the bird, the child will never see that bird again."

Jiddu Krishnamurti

Than all big figures starts to worry about my journey;

Preparation of life starts now onwards .

Like me ; many small figures gather at this place,

We call it a place of preparation .

All The straight figures are the mentors;

They are very caring and kind.

They want us to become like them.

This place is all about time table

When to eat

When to speak

When to read

When to learn

At first I hesitate to join ;

But I am very impressed by the place of preparation .

They teach all the necessary things for journey

Like

How to think

What to think

What to ask

How to spell

Now I have no worries about anything in journey ;

I think that's the blueprint of journey.

One by one upgrade happening ;

Becoming more and more prepare for journey.

Then one day ,

I spell wrong ;

I become sovereign of laughter .

Can’t draw a straight line;

Can’t match with other figures.

How foolish am I?

Can not follow simple rule.

Then I decode it;

Strictly following rules are the epitome of place of preparation.

Observe every figure,

Learn from every figure;

How to react

How to talk

What to wear.

Unbelievable

But now I am hero here ;

The hero with all observations skill

Collecting all reputable and good manners from surrounding.

Started flying in sky

First in rank

First to remember

First to answer.

Learning what is already learned ;

By seeing surrounding straight figures,

By obeying rules and regulations ,

By not crossing border .

Think according to the books;

Behave according to the place of preparation.

Now surrounding has more control over me,

Can not Scribble.

Who cares about Scribble ;

If I can draw straight line .

Perfect for journey. Period.

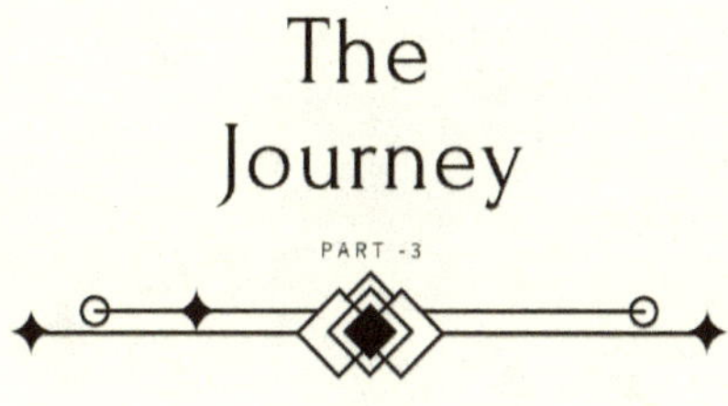
The
Journey
PART -3

“Life is what happens while you are busy making other plans.”

John Lennon

The witness

Ready to launch in journey;

Excited about future adventures.

Eyes sparkling,

Fitness at pick

Mind well prepared for dream.

Joins the institute of work;

Here also rules and regulations to follow,

But who can be better follower than me?

After passing place of preparation with first class.

Work at office,

Talk with friends ,

Party at house.

Work at office,

Talk with family,

Party at bar.

Work at office,

Talk with friends ,

Party at pub.

It become monotonous ;

Tired one day.

I decided to skip routine.

But

Skip routine

Skip formalities

Skip line . It's sin here.

That suffocate me,

What am I becoming ?

I am upset.

Then I find love companion

Who is perfect for me

Her superior guidance in everything;

Does not allow to show imperfections in me .

Become happy ,

Journey will be fantastic.

After sometimes,

Her guidance become new routine for me.

What to show

What to know

How to speak.

Realising ,

I can't become perfect for this journey ;

I started searching for my own train.

Searching Every corner ,

Reading Every book.

For my journey my train.

Once I heard about a cult at institute ;

Become enthusiastic to join it.

Cult is very nice and very rich of discipline

There I met a big figure

His every sentences will become quotes in future book.

I joined;

Hope to find my own journey.

We have ritual ,

We have method to do things,

We are disciplined in every manner .

We try to impress supreme figure ;

Big figure already impressed that one .

Can’t break ritual

It’s sin to cult

I follow ritual ;

everyday and every moment;

Again all Seems to monotonous .

The same ;

Office become hut ,

Work become ritual .

Depressed with my nature

Non compatible with other figures.

Lastly I know that

Relaxation is not my ritual.

The Departure

PART -4

" The only way to make sense out of changes to plunge into it, move with it, and join the dance"

Alan Watts

At

Time of tiredness when relaxation is not possible.

Walking at beach ;

Tears rolling .

Infinity of ocean grasps me.

In deep down ;

Suffocating with unsatisfactory nature.

Can’t bearing burden of journey .

Incompetent.

Weird.

Unmatched.

That are words used for me .

I tried my best in every situation ;

But dissatisfaction, misery and anxiety for being perfect haunt me.

Finally I sat at seashore for listening the sound of ocean;

The magnificent ocean,

Seems to told me ‘ Hold my bear’.

I saw a shadow of a man emerging from ocean;

With my teary eyes,

I can not see precisely but he seems malformed with limbs.

He walks towards me ;

I turn my face the other side.

He blubber something;

He wants to talk

But I am not interested .

He tries a lot ;

But I don't give attention.

Dropping his hope he walked out of there.

Ignorance of me ; poking my heart .

Lastly I speak,

'What? Who are you?'

'The witness.' he answered and sat beside me.

'Witness of what ?'

'Your.'

'Hahahaha, witness of me ?'

'This is not the best time for joke.'

I laughed.

He also laughed ;

He has a brilliant smile .

He has Blissful eyes , I noted lastly.

'What happened?' He asked.

Hesitate, but I answered

'I failed at preparation'

‘For what are you preparing?’

‘For journey’ I answer.

‘**Hahahaha...**’ he laughs.

It irritates me.

'You are already prepared for journey that's why you are in.' he answers

'Then why Am I not enjoying the journey?'

'Because you are always engage in your preparation for journey '

‘Ok, then what is your advice to enjoy?’ I reply with evil laugh.

‘Forget about your past and forget about your future preparation. Live in the present’

‘Why is living in the present moment so important?’My laugh wearing off.

'Because living in present moment saves your energy. Your past and future thoughts drain your energy'

'Got it. But how can I live in present moments? Any method? Any ritual to follow?'

'Hahahaha... poor fellow. Always wants to follow or to be followed'

'Just throw your ego. Ego is the biggest enemy of present. And you will find yourself in bliss'

' My dear friend, I am egoless person. I am down to earth person ask anyone here.' I answer proudly

'Ok then why are you suffering? Why is there so much void in your life ?'

'I am suffering because I am not competitive enough for institute, cult or companion.'

'But who says you are not competitive enough?'

'My surrounding figures said that.'

'Have you seen yourself in mirror?What mirror actually show?'

'Yes, mirror show which is stand forefront to it.'

'Wrong; Have you seen the different types of mirrors? Like if you stand before it. It will show tall of you, short of you and obese of you according to types of mirror?'

'Yes , I have seen it. Mirrors actually show its characteristics not a standing man front of it.'

'Absolutely, the cult , companion and institute are just different types of mirror which shows their characteristics'

'Then what about marks and ranks which show me that I am not competitive?'

'It's just comparison which is the root cause of ego. Your ego don't want to rest your mind it is always comparing with others. So you can always remain in vivid imagination of your past or future'

'Sorry to say but if I don't prepare then what about my future journey?'

'Trust your present moment. Enjoy your present moment. It will automatically lead to your destination.'

'How can I live in present moment if my future is not secure?'

'Just create non-attachment for past and future, doing and non doing, pass and fail.'

'Easily said but I am a human being . How can I detach so easily'

'Just remind your self that you are not body, you are not mind you are beyond that then non attachment becomes easy'

'Oh sorry brother but here you are wrong. If I will detach myself then how can I enjoy present?'

'Actually non attachment makes you more blissful in present moment. Non attachment does not mean vairagya.If you accept whatever fall before you then you enjoy more than before. That's paradox of non attachment '

'How ?'

'Acceptance makes you free from desire. Acceptance avoids comparison. So ego goes ; blissfulness comes'

‘Then how can I live my life?’ I asked with cool mind.

‘Have you seen any movie drama ?’

‘Yes .’

‘How can you define best acting ?’

'Acting in which actor fully merged with his character in emotion and action'

'Yes right. You have to also merge in this journey with action and emotion but definitely remind yourself that this is just a drama , you are just playing your role.'

‘Yes, now I understand . As an actor don’t attach to his reel role for lifetime, we should not attach to play of our mind’

‘Very good, and acceptance of role in life like drama . Everybody wants to be hero ? Nobody wants to be villain? Then play never happens.’

‘If we accept our role and play then we enjoy our performance more blissfully’ I complete his metaphor with smile.

'That's paradox of non attachment we discussed before' he answered and he stood up ; simply wants to end discussion.

'Thank you .' My eyes sparkled with new insights.

He just smiled.

'Can I ask you one last question?'

'Yes of course.'

'The most basic question, if you don't want to answer then ok. Because most of the philosophical books and person tried it . But never get it.'

'Just ask the question.'

'Who am I?'

'Have you like the metaphor of drama ?'

'Yes.'

'You are not a scene of drama ; you are not a audience.'

'You are not a vista; you are not a spectator.'

'You are really a witness of both.'

'You are drasta; you are witness here.'

'You are not a body ; you are not a mind.'

'You are beyond that.'

'You are witness.'

'You are witness of yourself.'

'You are witness of all.'

'You are part of all.'

'You are all.'

I don't remember him answering or I am speaking ;

Only listening or realising those words;

Reel of my journey from arrival to end passing through my eyes.

Becoming witness of my journey ;

I am happy and joyful .

Blissfulness poured upon me .

I am in the present moment of existence.

****

www.ingramcontent.com/pod-product-compliance
Lightning Source LLC
LaVergne TN
LVHW041103150826
845673LV00007B/1895

9798892336895